JOHN A. HOWE BRANCH
ALBANY PUBLIC LIBRARY

W9-AHY-933

DESIGN BY YVETTE LENHART

EGMONT
we bring stories to life

First published by Egmont USA, 2009
443 Park Avenue South, Suite 806
New York, NY 10016

Text copyright © 2009 Walter Dean Myers
Illustrations copyright © 2009 Christopher Myers
All rights reserved

10 9 8 7 6 5 4 3 2 1

www.egmontusa.com
www.walterdeanmyers.net

LIBRARY OF CONGRESS CATALOGING-IN-PUBLICATION DATA

Myers, Walter Dean, 1937 –
Looking like me / by Walter Dean Myers; illustrated by Christopher Myers.
p. cm.

Summary: Jeremy sets out to discover all of the different "people" that make him who he is,
including brother, son, writer, and runner.

ISBN 978-1-60684-001-6 (hardcover picture book) – ISBN 978-1-60684-041-2 (reinforced library
binding) [1. Individuality—Fiction. 2. Family life—New York (State)—Harlem—Fiction. 3. African
Americans—Fiction. 4. Harlem (New York, N.Y.)—Fiction.] I. Myers, Christopher, ill. II. Title.

PZ7.M992Loo 2009
[E]—dc22
2009014640

CPSIA tracking label information: Printed in Singapore by CS Graphics · Date of Production:
August 17, 2009 · Cohort: Batch 1

All rights reserved. No part of this publication may be reproduced, stored in a retrieval
system, or transmitted, in any form or by any means, electronic, mechanical, photocopying,
or otherwise, without the prior permission of the publisher and copyright owner.

LOOKING LIKE ME

BY WALTER DEAN MYERS

ILLUSTRATED BY CHRISTOPHER MYERS

EGMONT

USA | New York

I LOOKED IN THE MIRROR
AND WHAT DID I SEE?
A REAL HANDSOME DUDE
LOOKING JUST LIKE ME.

ALONG CAME MY SISTER,

FINE AS SHE CAN BE.

"HEY, JEREMY," SHE SAID,

"YOU'RE LITTLE
BROTHER TO ME."

SHE PUT OUT HER FIST.

I GAVE IT A BAM!

JEREMY AND BROTHER,
THAT'S WHO I AM.

ALONG CAME MY FATHER.

HE SAID, "HAVING FUN?

BECAUSE IF YOU ARE,

YOU NEED TO ADD SON."

HE PUT OUT HIS FIST.

I GAVE IT A BAM!

I'M JEREMY, BROTHER, AND MY FATHER'S SON.

I GOT A
STRANGE
FEELING
I WASN'T
HALF DONE

"AREN'T YOU A WRITER?"

ASKED MY TEACHER, MISS KAY.

"I SAW YOU WRITING IN YOUR BOOK TODAY."

"I'M A WRITER,
SPINNING DRAMAS
THAT DANCE ACROSS THE STAGE,
A POET WEAVING MYSTERIES
THAT LIVE UPON THE PAGE."

MISS KAY PUT OUT HER FIST.

I GAVE IT A BAM!

SAY JEREMY,
SAY BROTHER,
SAY SON,
SAY WRITER,
THAT'S WHO I AM.

I'M WALKING TALL AND
I'M WALKING PROUD.
LOOKED IN THE MIRROR—

I LOOK LIKE
A CROWD.

"YOU'RE
A CITY
CHILD."

MY SKINNY
MAILMAN
GRINNED.

"AND I SEE
YOU'RE
REALLY
LOVING
THE CITY
THAT
YOU'RE IN."

"I'M A CITY CHILD. I LOVE THE DIZZY HEIGHTS, THE CONCRETE, THE STEEL, THE BRIGHT NEON LIGHTS."

THE MAILMAN
LIFTED HIS FIST.

I GAVE IT
A BAM!

IT IS KIND OF AMAZING
ALL THE PEOPLE I AM.

"YOU'RE AN "

SAID MY GRANDMA.

"YOUR PICTURES MAKE ME SMILE. I LOVE YOUR FUNNY PORTRAITS, AND YOUR SCENES HAVE SO MUCH STYLE!"

GRANDMA'S RINGS AND BANGLES GAVE SUCH A NOISY

 **BAM!**

THEY WERE REALLY CELEBRATING THE KIND OF GUY I AM.

"I KNOW THAT YOU'RE A DANCER," SAID A SWEET GIRL WHIRLING BY.

"YOU MOVE YOUR FEET TO A SALSA BEAT

WITH A TWINKLE IN YOUR EYE."

SHE PUT OUT
HER FIST.

I GAVE
IT A
BAM!

I ADDED DANCER
TO THE ANSWER
OF JUST WHO I AM

I KNOW THAT I'M A TALKER WITH MANY TALES TO TELL.

JOKES AND NEWS AND SECRETS — I HOPE I TELL THEM WELL.

MY WORDS ARE SOMETIMES HURRIED; AT TIMES THEY COME OUT SLOW.

AT TIMES THEY FLY LIKE SNOWFLAKES WITH EVERYWHERE TO GO.

SOMETIMES I
LET MY WORDS
GO FREE,
LIKE MARBLES
OFF A SHELF.

SOMETIMES I
GIVE MYSELF A
BAM
AND KEEP THEM
TO MYSELF.

I SAW KAREN RUNNING,
SO I RAN, TOO.
SHE SAID, "HEY, JEREMY.
WHAT'S UP WITH YOU?"

I SAID, "I'M A RUNNER.

I JUST LOVE TO RACE

WITH THE SPINNING EARTH

BENEATH ME, THE WIND

BLOWING IN MY FACE."

I GAVE IT A BAM!

WHEN SHE PUT OUT HER FIST.

THEN I ADDED RUNNER TO MY "I AM" LIST.

MY MOM CALLS
ME A DREAMER,

A SILVER-RAYED MOONBEAMER,

SPREADING FANTASIES ACROSS

THE HARLEM SKY.

I DREAM OF SECRET PLACES,

PLAID CLOUDS AND HIDDEN FACES,

BLACK KNIGHTS AND MAIDS

WHO SWOON AND SIGH.

MY MOM PUT OUT HER FIST.

I GAVE IT A GENTLE BAM,

BECAUSE THAT'S THE KIND OF

DREAMER THAT I AM.

WHY DON'T
YOU FIND
A MIRROR
AND SOME
FRIENDS
ALONG THE
WAY?

THINK OF
ALL THE
THINGS
YOU DO
AND ALL
THE THINGS
THEY SAY.

MAKE A
LONG LIST IF
YOU WANT
TO — HAVE
YOURSELF
AN "I AM"
JAM.

THEN GIVE
YOURSELF
A GREAT BIG
SMILE AND
YOUR FIST
A GREAT BIG

BAM!

ABOUT THE AUTHOR AND ILLUSTRATOR

We've looked in the mirror and what did we see? Two handsome dudes and a

BOY

SON

BROTHER

READER

FRIEND

DANCER

CLASSMATE

PAINTER

POET

WRITER

SCULPTOR

ATHLETE

STUDENT

COLLEGE GRADUATE

COLLECTOR

FLUTE PLAYER

Walter

SPEAKER

PHOTOGRAPHER

Christopher

COLLAGIST

DREAMER